the Fifolet

Written by Johnette Downing

Illustrated by Jennifer Lindsley

PELICAN PUBLISHING COMPANY

GRETNA 2015

For Scott, the light of my life—J. D.

*The word "Pelican" and the depiction of a pelican are
trademarks of Pelican Publishing Company, Inc., and are
registered in the U.S. Patent and Trademark Office.*

ISBN 9781455620364
E-book ISBN 9781455620371

Printed in Malaysia
Published by Pelican Publishing Company, Inc.
1000 Burmaster Street, Gretna, Louisiana 70053

THE FIFOLET
Deep in the swamp under the pale moonlight
lives a Cajun legend that will give you a fright.

Through the cypress trees and beards of moss,
there is a fire sprite that you never want to cross.
It will tease you and coax you and draw you near,
but all the Cajuns know that you better beware.

No matter the warnings,
it is hard to resist,

because wherever you see it, treasures exist.

Trappers and fishermen will tell you the same;
a fifolet is a ball of light, a dancing blue flame.

And so the story goes year after year: if you follow the fifolet, you just may disappear.

There once was a fisherman named Jean-Paul Pierre.
In Atchafalaya, he had a shack there.

It rested on the water like so many before.
He had a wooden pirogue tied near the shore.

Every morning before the
sun met the sky,

Jean-Paul would start fishing until the moon was high.

He had no time for family and no time for friends.
He fished and fished, from daybreak till day ends.
He shared his catch with no one; greed ran in his veins.
Like so many vices, his greed still remains.
Here is where the story of the fifolet begins,
but for Jean-Paul Pierre, the story never ends.

One night Jean-Paul was catching
beaucoup—many—fish,

but Jean-Paul was greedy, so
more was his wish.

He fished all the next day and into the night,
until in the distance he saw a dancing light.

"A dancing light," he thought. "How can that be?"
Then he recalled the warning when a fifolet you see.

His body began to tremble
with a fear he could not shake,

but the fifolet was enticing; its
spell he could not break.

Its bouncing light was playful, a rhythmic, flowing trance;
it glistened on black water and flickered through each branch.

Jean-Paul paddled closer then quickly rowed away.
"The fifolet will get you," he heard himself say.

He paddled his pirogue faster
until he made it home,

and in his bed that night, his thoughts
began to roam.

He remembered the fifolet, beautiful against the night:

a swaying, undulating, blazing blue light.

Then all of a sudden he sat straight up in bed.
The thought of the treasure popped into his head.

"Where you see a fifolet, treasure
is sure to be."

He thought and thought of this
and could not set it free.

Back into his boat he went and
paddled with great speed.

He abandoned all his fears,
driven only by his greed.

When he reached the spot where
he had seen the fifolet,

the moon was bowing
to yet another day.

Out of the boat with his shovel, he began to dig.
Like the fifolet, his movements were that of a jig.
Every day and every night he dug for buried treasure.
He is still digging there, much to the fifolet's pleasure.

Just as legend tells, Jean-Paul Pierre disappeared forever.

As for the fifolet, there are now two, and they are twice as clever.